Echo and the Bat Pack

THE PIRATE WITH THE GOLDEN TOOTH

text by Roberto Pavanello
translated by Marco Zeni

Raintree

Raintree is an imprint of Capstone Global Library Limited, a company incorporated in England and Wales having its registered office at 7 Pilgrim Street, London, EC4V 6LB – Registered company number: 6695582

To contact Raintree:
Phone: 0845 6044371
Fax: + 44 (0) 1865 312263
Email: myorders@raintreepublishers.co.uk
Outside the UK please telephone +44 1865 312262.

Text by Roberto Pavanello
Original cover and illustrations by Blasco Pisapia and Pamela Brughera
Graphic Project by Laura Zuccotti and Gioia Giunchi

© 2008 Edizioni Piemme S.p.A., via Tiziano 32 - 20145 Milano- Italy
International Rights © Atlantyca S.p.A., via Leopardi, 8 — 20123 Milano, Italy — foreignrights@atlantyca.it
Original Title: IL MAMMUT FREDDOLOSO
Translation by: Marco Zeni

First published by Stone Arch Books © 2013
First published in the United Kingdom in 2013
The moral rights of the proprietor have been asserted.

Printed and bound in China by CTPS

ISBN 978 1 4062 6200 1 (paperback)
17 16 15 14 13
10 9 8 7 6 5 4 3 2 1

CONTENTS

Hello there!

I'm your friend Echo, here to tell you about one of the Bat Pack's adventures!

Do you know what I do for a living? I'm a writer, and scary stories are my speciality. Creepy stories about witches, ghosts, and graveyards. But I'll tell you a secret – I am a real scaredy-bat!

First of all, let me introduce you to the Bat Pack. These are my friends. . . .

Becca

Age: 10

Loves all animals (especially bats!)

Excellent at bandaging broken wings

Michael

Age: 12

Clever, thoughtful, and good at solving problems

Doesn't take no for an answer

Tyler

Age: 11

Computer genius

Funny and adventurous, but scared of his own shadow

Dear fans of scary stories,

As you probably already know (and if you don't, I'm telling you), bats have a terrific sense of direction. We never lose our bearings. Have you heard that saying before? If you've lost your bearings, it means you're lost and can't find your way.

Until now, that had never happened to me. I had never mistaken my legs for my wings, not even after performing the Death Loop, the most difficult stunt for any bat! We bats don't even need to carry a compass. We have one in our head, and it works like a charm!

Well, most of the time, at least. But if, by chance, you happen to bump into the world's most beautiful bat and the worst compass in all the seven seas at the same time, everything goes a little haywire!

That's exactly what happened to me when I went on a trip to the beach with the Silver kids. They dragged me into yet another scary adventure, and for the first time ever, I lost my bearings!

Mint-flavoured worms

The train was right on time. In fifteen minutes, we would be at the beach!

I couldn't wait. I had never seen the sea. As a matter of fact, I had never even been on a train. If I'm being completely honest, I have to confess that I'd never even been on holiday before!

What was I doing there with the Silver kids then? It's simple. Uncle Charlie, one of Mrs Silver's brothers, had invited them to come and stay at his house for a week.

Chapter 1

Michael and Tyler had been thrilled and immediately said yes. Becca was the only one who thought of me. "If Echo isn't coming, I'm not going anywhere!" she insisted.

She's so thoughtful! Although, thinking back on it now, if I had known what kind of mess I was about to get myself into, I might not have gone anywhere in the first place.

"I hope I remember what Uncle Charlie looks like," Becca said, bringing my attention back to the present.

"I remember!" Tyler said. "He has a single eye in the middle of his forehead and has yellow slobber dribbling out of his huge mouth!"

"Yellow slobber?" I asked worriedly.

"Don't listen to him, Echo," Michael reassured me. "Uncle Charlie is really nice. He's just . . . well . . . a little different."

"What do you mean, 'different'?" I asked.

"I just mean that he's not really interested in what other people think about him," Michael explained. "He just kind of does his own thing. And he's really into old stuff, like antiques. You'll see what I mean when you see his house."

I decided to stop asking questions. Maybe I was better off not knowing.

* * *

Several minutes later we got off at Portwind's old train station.

That's when I finally understood what the children meant by "different." Waiting for us next to an antique car stood a tall, lanky man with a thick moustache. He was wearing a long trench coat, a leather helmet, and a pair of big goggles.

As soon as he saw us, he ran towards us with his arms open.

"Welcome ashore, sailors!" he called. "How was your cruise? Did the southwesterly winds keep you company?"

Then, without waiting for us to reply, he grabbed our bags, threw them into the boot of the car, and motioned for us to hop in. The moment he started the car, we were covered by a cloud of black smoke.

"Ah, my old Tripper!" he said proudly as we all coughed, trying to breathe through the smoke. "She's only 84 years old and still running like a beauty! Right full rudder! Aye!"

Uncle Charlie stepped on the accelerator and the car zoomed off, accelerating until it reached its top speed – twenty miles per hour!

"Amazing, isn't she?" Uncle Charlie beamed, turning around. That's when he caught sight of me. His eyes practically bulged out of his head.

"What is that?" he demanded. He continued to drive facing backwards.

"He's my pet bat!" Becca replied. "His name is Echo, and he's a writer!"

"Um . . . I think you should turn around now, Uncle Charlie!" Michael said nervously. We were fast approaching an enormous tree.

"Turn around? Oh, of course, good idea!" Uncle Charlie replied. He turned around at the last minute, narrowly avoiding a collision with the tree. Uncle Charlie seemed unconcerned, while Tyler turned white as a sheet.

"A writer, you said?" Charlie asked, turning around again.

"Sure, and he can talk, too," Becca said.

"Uncle Charlie, watch the bend!" Michael yelled again.

"Bend? What bend?" Charlie asked, miraculously managing to stay on the road.

Tyler was growing paler and paler by the second.

"You'll find some good inspiration for your writing in Portwind, Echo!" Charlie assured me, looking at me instead of watching the road.

"WATCH THE TRAIN, UNCLE CHARLIE!!"
Michael suddenly shouted. "THE TRAAAIN!!!"

"What train?" Charlie asked, turning around
abruptly.

A huge train was running at full speed towards
the unattended level crossing.

I closed my eyes, certain that my time had

come. *Dying like this – what a shame*, I thought. *I wish I could have seen the ocean at least once!*

When I opened my eyes again, we were somehow on the other side of the tracks. The train whistled as it sped away from us.

The old clunker started up a slight hill. I was almost afraid to look. What near miss would be waiting for us on the other side?

But when we reached the top, the most beautiful scene I had ever laid eyes upon opened up before us. Shining beneath the sun, a blue blanket sprawled as far as the eye could see, broken only by the occasional white wave. Wow!

"Is that the ocean?" I asked excitedly.

"It is indeed! And that," Uncle Charlie added, "is my house!"

Chapter 2

Creepy legends

Uncle Charlie's house was in even worse shape than his car. It was an old stone villa, complete with a pointed tower, that the adventurous architect had decided to build right on the edge of a cliff.

"Welcome to my humble abode!" Uncle Charlie bellowed, throwing his helmet and goggles in the air. "Be careful climbing the stairs. They lean to the right a bit."

He led us up a narrow spiral staircase. Michael,

Tyler, and Becca
followed, dragging
their suitcases
behind them.

I decided to take
the lift (my wings, I
mean) and got to the
first floor in the blink
of an eye.

I found myself in
a room that looked
like a cross between
a maritime museum
and a landfill site.
There were oil
lamps, stacks of
old books, various
wooden masks, old
ship models, flags

belonging to missing boats, and even a skull with glowing eyes.

"What an . . . interesting place!" I muttered politely.

"Thank you!" Uncle Charlie said, continuing up the spiral staircase. "Come along, children! Your room is right at the top of the tower!"

"Oh, that's just great!" Tyler grunted, struggling to haul his suitcase up the winding stairs.

When we finally reached the top of the tower, I had to admit that the view was worth the long climb.

"What's that, Uncle Charlie?" Michael asked. He pointed at something across the water. Whatever it was was hidden by a thick layer of fog. "It looks like an island."

"That's because it *is* an island," his uncle

replied. "Anyway, I think we'd better go back downstairs. Aren't you hungry?"

"I am!" Tyler replied quickly.

But Michael wasn't so easily distracted. "Is it always surrounded by fog?" he asked.

"What? Oh, the island, you mean?" his uncle said. "Um, yes, I suppose it is. You know, there are some weird rumours about that island . . ." Uncle Charlie stopped. "But never mind. Let's go to the kitchen and I'll make you kids a snack. Who's coming?"

"I AM!!!" Tyler said again.

"Hang on, Tyler," Michael insisted. "Aren't you the least bit interested in knowing what the rumours about that island are?"

"Of course," Tyler replied. "It's my stomach that doesn't care."

"Don't listen to him, Uncle Charlie," Becca said, rolling her eyes. "Tell us about it."

"Oh, it's all just a bunch of nonsense," their uncle said. "According to legend, the island is haunted by a crew of ghost pirates!"

"Really?" Michael replied, looking wide-eyed and very interested.

"Supposedly, their ship crashed against those rocks over there," Uncle Charlie said, pointing at a large outcropping of rocks across the water. "It seems that a curse struck both the pirates and the island itself. That's why it's always hidden by fog." He shook his head. "Ridiculous, isn't it? Well. Are you kids hungry or not?"

"I think I've lost my appetite," Tyler muttered miserably.

"Does anybody know what kind of curse it is?" I asked. Considering how interested Michael seemed, I figured it was better to know what we were getting into.

"Oh, there are plenty of ideas, but it's just a load of gobbledy-gook, I'm sure," Uncle Charlie replied.

"Have you ever been over there?" Michael asked.

"Oh, I'll be honest, I've thought about going over there plenty of times," Uncle Charlie admitted. "You know how much I like old stories about sailors. But I don't feel comfortable going there on my own, and I've never found anyone who wanted to go with me. People here are too scared of Skull Island!"

The room fell silent.

"Is . . . is that its name?" Tyler asked, turning white as a ghost again.

"Yes," Uncle Charlie said. "At least that's what people around here call it."

"Why?" I asked.

"Because it's shaped like a skull, at least according to the few brave men who've been there," Uncle Charlie told me. "Come on now, do you want that snack or not?"

"Actually, I'm not hungry anymore," Tyler said without taking his eyes off the ocean. "But maybe something sweet will make me feel better."

"No sweets here," Uncle Charlie said cheerfully. "Us sea folk only eat fish!"

Chapter 3

One-legged sailor

The following morning, Uncle Charlie woke us up very early, shouting, "All hands on deck! Everyone below deck!"

"What time is it?" Tyler asked, yawning widely. He was clearly not a morning person. I could appreciate that.

"Six thirty!" Becca replied cheerfully. She was already dressed and ready to start the day. "Come on, lazybones!"

I felt like I needed a pair of toothpicks to hold

my eyes open! When are you humans going to understand that bats are creatures of the night?

"It's market day today! The earlier you go, the fresher the fish will be!" Uncle Charlie said, shoving two fried fish fillets under my nose.

Fish as an afternoon snack was one thing. But for breakfast, lunch, and dinner, too? That was a nightmare! Bats don't like fish. I mean, I prefer fruit flies!

We all ate very little before piling back into Uncle Charlie's car and heading off to the market. I fell asleep aboard old Tripper. When I woke up among the market stalls, I was overwhelmed by the familiar smell of fish.

"This way, sailors," Uncle Charlie commanded. "I have to see an old friend first!" He led us through a maze of crowded stalls before stopping in front of a small shop. A sign hanging at the front read, "The Short-Sighted Helmsman."

Uncle Charlie walked into the shop. Inside, we discovered all sorts of marine antiques. I even spotted a stuffed bat in the window!

Tyler's joke was right on time. "Look at that, Echo! Think that's a relative of yours?"

Suddenly an old man appeared and limped towards us. He had a wooden leg.

"Children, meet my friend, Cornelius Chips,"
Uncle Charlie said. "He's Portwind's most
experienced sailor. And these, my dear Cornelius,
are my niece and nephews. Meet Michael, Tyler,
and Becca. That little fellow hiding behind them is
Echo, their bat."

"A live bat!" the old man said with surprise.
"Have you ever thought of having him stuffed?"

Everyone laughed, except me. I didn't see what
was so funny about that!

"Go ahead and have a look around, kids,"
Uncle Charlie suggested.

The Silver kids started browsing around the
shop, inspecting the knick-knack-filled shelves.
I fluttered after them, making sure to stay well
away from that old sailor.

"Hey, have a look at this!" Michael exclaimed,

blowing the dust off a big book. "It's *The Darkest Legends of the Sea* by Edgar Allan Poultry!"

Cornelius wandered over and joined us, rubbing his hands together. "With that, you'll finally solve the mystery of Skull Island!" he said. "Ha, ha, ha! Has your uncle told you about it yet?"

"He mentioned the legend," Michael replied. "But he wouldn't tell us any of the details."

"Legend?" Cornelius repeated. "He told you it's just a legend? But, Charlie . . ."

"Cornelius," Uncle Charlie interrupted him, "don't be filling their heads with that nonsense! Today's kids are easily impressed, you know that."

He obviously doesn't know the Silver kids! I thought to myself.

Before Cornelius could tell us more, Uncle

Charlie shooed us out of the
shop. He bought the book for
Michael and wanted to buy
a gift for each of us –
even me! I chose a
beautiful quill feather
to write my stories with,

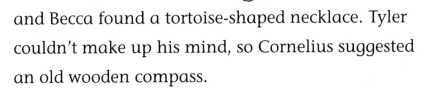

and Becca found a tortoise-shaped necklace. Tyler
couldn't make up his mind, so Cornelius suggested
an old wooden compass.

"But the needle is crooked!" Tyler complained,
inspecting it.

"Yes, it is," Cornelius replied, "but when you're
looking for somewhere that's hidden, standard
directions may not be enough!"

Tyler smiled without understanding what the
man meant. He kept the compass anyway.

* * *

"Your friend seemed nice, Uncle Charlie," Tyler said as soon as we were out of the shop. "What happened to his leg?"

"He had an argument with a shark once," Uncle Charlie replied.

Tyler gulped. "You're saying that the shark ate his . . ."

"That's right!" his uncle replied. "We eat fish, but sometimes fish will eat us! Funny, isn't it?"

"Yeah, right . . . very funny," Tyler stuttered.

"Okay! Follow me, my fellow sailors!" Uncle Charlie commanded. "Fresh fish doesn't wait!" With that, he took off, striding purposely towards old Tripper.

Chapter 4

Smells like trouble!

It was lunchtime by the time we arrived back at Uncle Charlie's house.

"You'll have to entertain yourselves for a bit. I can't be disturbed now!" Uncle Charlie warned us as he headed into the kitchen. "My fish soup requires all of my concentration!"

I decided to take advantage of the free time to have a nap. I hung from the chandelier, while the children assembled in the living room. Michael started skimming through his new book.

I had just closed my eyes when I heard him shout, "Hey! Have a look at this!"

I sighed. *So much for my nap!* I thought.

I fluttered down from the chandelier, and we all gathered around Michael to have a look at what he'd found. An old piece of parchment paper showing a skull-shaped island had slipped out of the book. It showed a huge cave, and in the background, you could just make out the shape

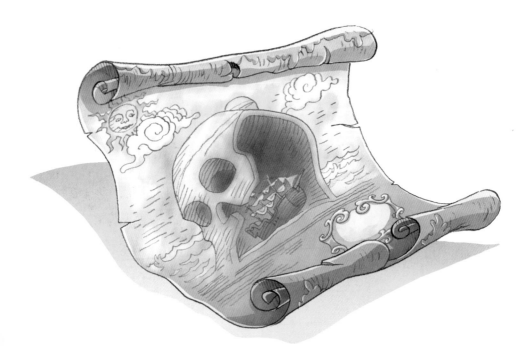

of a half-wrecked sailing ship. Below the drawing were two words half rubbed out: **SK-L- I-L-ND**

"Skull Island!" I blurted out.

"Bingo!" Michael confirmed. "But what is this old map doing in my book?"

"I don't like this one bit," Tyler said. "It smells like trouble."

"The fish soup, you mean?" Michael asked, folding up the map.

"Of course I don't mean the soup!" Tyler exclaimed. "I mean the . . ."

But before he could finish his sentence, he was interrupted by Uncle Charlie calling us for lunch.

As it turned out, the fish soup was delicious. It might have been the atmosphere, but even I had a second helping!

We all helped with the washing up, and then headed up to our room to get some rest.

I finally managed to hang from the ceiling and look at the world from the right perspective – upside down, obviously.

Becca tried on her new necklace, while Michael immersed himself in reading Edgar Allan Poultry's book. Tyler was busy banging his new compass on the floor, trying to get the needle to move. I was just about to doze off when Michael interrupted yet again.

"It's all true!" he yelled.

"What's true?" I asked sleepily, reluctantly opening my eyes.

"The legend Uncle Charlie told us about," Michael said. "Listen to this. 'The year was 1666. On the night of the 17th of April, off the coast of Skull Island, near Portwind, the famous pirate Goldtooth's infamous vessel, the *Ramshackle,* was seen sailing in the neighbouring

waters. Following the directions on an unclear map, the captain was searching for a mysterious treasure that was hidden beneath those treacherous waters.'"

Except for the treasure map, the legend confirmed what Uncle Charlie had told us. The ship had been wrecked, and nobody had ever known what had become of it and its crew!

"By my grandpa's sonar!" I gasped. "What a story!"

"Wait a minute," Tyler interrupted. "Who says the story is even true?"

Michael looked his brother straight in the eye. "The great Edgar Allan Poultry, that's who. He never lies!"

"Come on," Tyler said, sounding more and more nervous. "Don't tell me you believe that story."

"Let's say the book is telling the truth," Becca said, trying to keep the peace. "We still don't have any evidence."

"We could find some evidence!" Michael said.

Tyler and I looked at each other. We were both smelling trouble now!

"You're not thinking what I think you're thinking, are you?" Tyler asked.

"If you're thinking we need to go to that island, then you're right!" Michael said.

"I knew it!" Tyler exclaimed. "I come to the

beach thinking of relaxing and working on my tan, and I end up chasing ghosts instead! Do you know what I think? I think you'll never find anyone who'll take you to the island. You heard what Uncle Charlie said, didn't you?"

"I wasn't thinking of asking Uncle Charlie," Michael replied, just as his glasses fogged up.

Tyler and I looked at each other again. There was no doubt about it now. Fogged-up glasses meant trouble was on its way!

Chapter 5

Stockfish and mist

Who was Michael thinking of? Cornelius Chips, of course!

The next day, after a breakfast of grilled calamari (squid, ewww!), Uncle Charlie gave us the chance to go back to town. For some reason, when he came downstairs, he was dressed as an Eskimo. He must have noticed the weird looks we were giving him because he explained his choice of outfit.

"I have been invited to the annual meeting

of the Friends of Alaska Club," he told us. "I'll be gone all day. But since it's so beautiful outside, I thought I could drop you kids off at Portwind's beach. It's a great place to have some fun! What do you think?"

"What about lunch?" Tyler asked, sounding deeply concerned.

"Don't worry! I made a surprise basket for you," Uncle Charlie said. "Now are you ready to raise anchor and set sail, sailors?"

"Let's go!" the Silver kids answered in unison.

"Let's stay here," I whispered, but nobody heard me.

* * *

After Uncle Charlie dropped us off at the beach
and headed off to his meeting, we decided to split
into two groups. Michael was anxious to get some
answers about Skull Island, so he and I headed to
the Short-Sighted Helmsman to talk to Cornelius
Chips. Tyler and Becca stayed on the beach to bask
in the sun.

As soon as we stepped into the shop, Cornelius
limped towards us and greeted us warmly. "Ahoy,
Michael!" he said. "All by yourself this time?"

"Actually, Echo is here with me," Michael
replied.

"Oh, the bat!" Cornelius said. "You know, I just
sold that stuffed one I had. Are you sure you don't
want to be stuffed as well?" he asked me. "I would
be honoured."

"I wouldn't be quite so honoured," I snapped.

"As you wish," Cornelius said, sounding disappointed. "What can I do for you?"

"Well, we read the legend about Skull Island," Michael began.

"I knew you'd like it!" Cornelius replied.

"You can say that again!" Michael confirmed. "Let's say someone wanted to find out if the legend is true . . ."

Cornelius just stared at us attentively. He was smiling, but didn't say anything.

"Maybe," Michael went on, "you could take us over there one of these days, say . . . this afternoon?"

Cornelius didn't seem at all surprised by Michael's request. In fact, he agreed immediately.

With that, Michael and I went back to the beach to tell Tyler and Becca the plan.

It was lunchtime by then, and Tyler had already devoured Uncle Charlie's "surprise" basket. What was in it? Fish, fish, and more fish. Let's just say I didn't mind missing the meal.

When Tyler found out about the meeting with Cornelius, he immediately lost his appetite. He tried to talk us out of going, but it was all in vain.

"What are we going to tell Uncle Charlie?" Tyler asked in a last-ditch attempt to keep us from going.

"We'll tell him that his old friend Cornelius took us fishing," Michael reassured him.

It seemed Tyler could sense when he was fighting a losing battle. With a sigh, he followed us as we headed off to meet Cornelius.

* * *

The sun was already low when our boat left the harbour. No one made a sound as Cornelius pointed the tiny vessel towards Skull Island.

Once our boat entered the mist surrounding the island, we could barely breathe.

Cornelius continued slowly, leaning over the edge of the boat. Every now and then he would turn left or right, dodging some large rocks only he had seen.

"How does he do that?" Tyler asked softly.

"He must know these waters like the back of his hand," Becca whispered.

"Or maybe he stole the sonar from his stuffed bat," I joked.

A few minutes later, the mist began to thin out, and the island appeared before us. The skull stared

towards the open sea, but it looked as if it could swallow us up. Scaredy-bat!

Cornelius docked the boat in a narrow inlet, and the Silver kids and I climbed out.

"Keep your eyes peeled, and make sure to keep away from the northern side," Cornelius warned us. "Before the tide is up, I'll call you back with this!" He held up a large horn.

"Aren't you coming?" Becca asked.

He shook his head. "My leg won't let me. Besides, I don't like wandering around here."

Tyler gulped. I could tell he wasn't keen on the idea either. Fortunately, the sun was about to set, and I was finally starting to feel at ease.

Chapter 6

Two small yellow eyes

My good feeling didn't last long. As soon as Michael started walking up the narrow trail that led to the top of the island, I felt the cold seep into my bones. The dark rocks looked like frozen stone giants, and the slimy tufts of grass felt like a witch's hair slithering against us.

Suddenly, I saw two small yellow eyes staring at me from inside a dark crevice.

"Look!" Becca yelled. "It's a turtle!"

She moved closer to the little animal, but it disappeared.

When we got to the top, the view of the sea above the layer of mist made me feel a little better.

Michael started sketching a map of the island on his notepad. Tyler tried to show some courage and walked a few steps away. He immediately ran back, screaming, "Help! A monster is chasing me!"

Scaredy-bat! Protected by its heavy armour, the "monster" slowly advanced towards us.

"It's just the little turtle we saw earlier!" Becca said. "Stop shouting! You're scaring it!"

"*I'm* scaring *it*?" Tyler repeated. "It tried to eat me alive!"

"Oh, get a grip! Can't you see how small it is?" Becca replied. She gently picked up the animal and scratched its wrinkly neck. I have to admit, all

that cuddling made me feel a little jealous. It was
a stranger, after all!

"I'm going to call it Twinkle!" Becca declared.
"What do you think?"

"I think something isn't quite right," Michael
said, studying the animal. "How did it get up here
so quickly? It definitely didn't use the trail."

"What do you mean? You think it flew here?" Tyler asked. "Let's be serious now."

"Of course it didn't fly here," Michael said. "I mean there must be a secret passage. Echo, would you mind . . ."

"No way!" I replied, shaking my head. "I'm not moving from here!"

"Maybe the turtle can tell us," Becca suggested.

"Of course it can!" Tyler joked. "It's a real blabbermouth!"

"Not with words, you dummy!" Becca replied, rolling her eyes. She set the turtle on the ground. "Come on, Twinkle! Show us how you go back from here."

I know it's hard to believe, but the turtle did understand! It crawled into a dark crack between the rocks, and we followed it in single file.

"Tyler, do you have your torch?" Michael asked.

"Aha! You always come to me for help when you're up to your neck in trouble, don't you?!" Tyler said.

I heard a buzzing sound, and then a powerful light illuminated the tunnel. "Don't forget that the battery will only last for thirty minutes," Tyler warned us.

We continued crawling until the passage became too narrow to continue.

The turtle disappeared into it, but we couldn't go any further.

"End of the line!" Tyler said. "We kindly ask all passengers to go back, and try to be more intelligent next time!"

"What do we do now?" Becca asked. "We're stuck!"

Michael stared at me. "I know one of us who could keep going if he wanted to," he said.

I didn't say no straight away. First of all, because I didn't want to let my friends down. Secondly, because my ears had picked up on something coming from the other side of the opening.

"Shush!" I said. "Did you hear that too?"

"It's my stomach grumbling," Tyler said. "Sorry. I don't think Uncle Charlie's surprise basket agreed with me."

"It isn't that!" I said. "It's more like a whistling sound. It sounds like . . ."

"Pirates?" Tyler asked worriedly.

"Bats!" I bellowed, dashing into the dark hole.

Chapter 7

A professional dancer

It took all of my concentration to make my way through the tunnel without tearing my wings off in the process. It's just like my great-grandfather used to say, "When every single light is off, only clever bats can find a way out."

I flew past the turtle and ended up in a cave crowded with bats! One of them grabbed me and hugged me happily.

"Bartholomew!!!" the bat exclaimed. "We've

been expecting you! I'm your Uncle Procopius! Welcome to my daughter's birthday party!"

"Well, actually, I'm not . . ." I tried to say.

"Come on! Come and say hello to the others!" he said, patting me on the back.

Between brothers, sisters, cousins, nephews, grandparents, and great-grandparents, I had to kiss more than two hundred and fifty relatives that I had never met before!

"The birthday girl will be here in a minute," Procopius told me. "You'll start the dance, won't you? If memory serves me correctly, you're an excellent dancer!"

I was just about to excuse myself when the most beautiful creature I'd ever seen came gliding towards us. My jaw dropped to the floor, and I stood there, dumbstruck.

"There's my Lilly! Pretty, isn't she?" Procopius commented, nudging me.

By golly! I didn't know that a face that pretty could even exist!

"Dear friends!" Procopius exclaimed. "Lilly will start the party by dancing with her cousin Bartholomew, who's just flown in!"

Then he threw me into his daughter's arms. Her eyes were as blue as the sky!

"Hi, Barty!" she whispered. "You look different."

"Miss . . ." I stammered. "I'm not the person you think I am. And I have to tell you, I can't . . . uh . . . dance."

"Some things never change," Lilly said, laughing. "You're always the same old joker!"

I didn't even have time to reply, because I was pulled into the dance.

I was shocked when I managed to follow the steps! I even performed a couple of aerobatic stunts, earning some applause from the guests.

"You see? You're being modest as usual," Lilly said. "You're a great dancer!"

"Thank you," I replied. "But there's something I have to tell you."

"Whatever it is it can wait, Barty," Lilly insisted. "I have to blow out the candles now!"

Uncle Procopius forced me to have three large slices of cake and then dance with two fat aunts until I was out of breath.

Finally, Lilly came back to me. "Okay, Barty. What's the important thing you need to tell me?"

"Well . . . uh . . . it's just that . . . my name isn't Barty. It's Echo, and I'm not your cousin!"

"Echo?" Lilly repeated, flapping her long eyelashes. "Are you Casimir's grandson?"

"No!" I exclaimed. "I'm not part of your family! I got here by following a turtle."

"You mean Twinkle?" Lilly asked.

"What did you say?" I asked, flabbergasted. "That's the same name Becca gave him. Unbelievable!"

"Twinkle has been living here for at least one hundred years, and she knows every secret passage on this island," Lilly told me. "Thanks to her, we found this cave and the big one."

"The big one?" I repeated.

"You know, the big cave," Lilly said. "Where the shipwreck is."

"Goldtooth's ship?" I said, shocked. "So it's true, then?"

"Of course it is!" Lilly said, smiling at me. "People think it's a legend because no one's ever found the ship. But we know the way to the cave."

"Is there a way out as well?" I asked.

"Of course," she replied. "Once a year, Goldtooth's ship leaves the cave and sails out to sea. The pirates have the whole night to find the treasure they were looking for when they were shipwrecked. They haven't found it yet, but when they do, the spell that the captain and his crew prisoners are under will be broken. The pirates will leave, the fog will go away, and we'll finally be the only ones on this island!"

It didn't take me long to figure out that I had to seize this opportunity. "If you show me how to get into the big cave, my human friends and I might be able to help you get rid of the ghost pirates," I offered.

"Human friends?" Lilly repeated, looking scared.

"Don't worry," I said, trying to reassure her. "They're all very nice people. They won't hurt you!"

She stared at me with her big blue eyes. Finally she said, "Okay. Give me your hand!"

I was just about to hold out my hand when a shrill sound stopped me. It was Cornelius Chip's whistle!

"I have to go. My friends are calling me!" I told Lilly sadly. "I'll be back tomorrow, though, and we'll go to the big cave together."

"I'm counting on it," she replied. "Even if you aren't my cousin, I still like you!"

"I like you too!" I replied. Then I turned and flew back the way I'd come.

It was pitch black outside. Luckily, the Silver kids hadn't gone too far yet.

"Where on earth were you? We were so worried!" Becca scolded me.

"I have great news!" I told them.

"Great," Michael said, "but we'd better hurry

up and get out of here now before Cornelius leaves without us."

* * *

When we got to the dock below Uncle Charlie's house, we said goodbye to Cornelius and climbed up the ladder. As soon as we were in our room, Michael started pestering me.

"Well, Echo, you said you had great news. What is it?" he asked.

"I met a beautiful lady bat!" I exclaimed.

"Echo has a girlfriend! Echo has a girlfriend!" Tyler taunted me.

"That's it?" Michael asked, sounding irritated.

"That's just the beginning," I said.

I told them about the cave, about the curse, and about the plan to meet Lilly the next day.

"We have to come with you," Michael said.

"All that matters to me is that I don't get my bat friends into trouble," I said. "Especially Lilly."

"Echo has a girlfriend!" Tyler sang again.

"Let me take care of everything," Michael reassured me.

That evening at dinner, Michael put his plan in motion. "Uncle Charlie, we're all really curious about Skull Island. Do you think you could take us over there in your boat tomorrow?"

"Tomorrow? That's out of the question!" Uncle Charlie said. "I have to be at the Annual Meeting of the Seadogs. I'll be back very late. Besides, I already told you that Skull Island is no place to go exploring."

It seemed we had no choice but to let the subject drop. But if I knew Michael, he was already coming up with a backup plan.

* * *

The next day, Uncle Charlie came downstairs wearing his full Seadog uniform. He looked like a cross between a parrot and a sea-lion tamer. He reminded us he'd be home late, then left for his meeting.

I bet that the dock is the first place Michael will go, I thought to myself.

Sure enough, Michael went down to the dock, got in Uncle Charlie's boat, and made sure that the tank was full. Before dark, we would be back on Skull Island.

Chapter 8

An amazing pair of acrobats

Michael handled the boat like a pro. As soon as we hit the fog, he told me, "Go to the front of the boat, Echo! We need your sonar!"

That boy was clever! Who, besides me, a noble-winged dweller of the night, would be able to see through the fog?

When we finally docked on Skull Island, Tyler was so grateful that he dropped to his knees and kissed the ground. "I'm alive!" he exclaimed.

Suddenly, Becca began making strange sounds.

"Are you feeling ill?" I asked, alarmed.

"I told her she should have let me finish her fish!" Tyler said.

"Hush! I'm trying to call Twinkle," Becca said, sounding irritated.

And wouldn't you know it? A few minutes later, the little turtle popped up from among the stones and led us to the secret entrance.

When it got too narrow for my human friends to go any further, Michael turned to me. "It's up to you, Echo!" he said.

I nodded and flew into the tunnel, quickly reaching the bats' cave.

Lilly spotted me straight away. "You kept your promise!" she said. "Are you ready to see the big cave?"

Before I could respond, Lilly grabbed my wing. "Follow me!" she yelled.

With that, she turned and nosedived towards a crack in the rocky wall. She was very pretty and very reckless! At that moment, I was very grateful for flying lessons I'd had with my cousin Limp Wing, a member of the Aerobatic Display Team.

We flew through a narrow crevice, and at Lilly's signal, we drew a perfect semicircle in the air.

"Wow!" I said as we landed on the sand. "We make an amazing team!"

I looked around and realized I was in an enormous cave. In the centre, tilted to one side, stood a large wrecked ship. Goldtooth's ship!

The noise of rushing water made it hard for me to think.

"Where is that noise coming from?" I asked.

"Up there," Lilly replied, pointing to an opening in the cave. There was a waterfall on the outside.

"Where does it lead?" I asked.

"Outside. That's the skull's left eye!" Lilly said. "When the tide floods the cave, the ship floats up and reaches that opening. Then Goldtooth and his crew sail through it and out to sea."

"I have to tell my friends!" I exclaimed. "How can I get them down here?"

"There's only one way, but it's very dangerous,"

Lilly said. "They'll have to climb down the northern wall and go through the skull's eye!"

"That's absolutely impossible!" I gasped.

"If I help you, maybe it won't be," Lilly replied.

* * *

I should have known that the Silver kids wouldn't be discouraged by the difficult route.

"We're not going to be stopped by some measly wall!" Michael insisted when I told them how they'd have to get to Goldtooth's ship.

Tyler looked less sure. "But there's a waterfall!" he whined.

"So we'll get a bit wet," Michael said. "What's the problem?"

"But there are ghost pirates!" Tyler said.

"That's exactly why we're here," Michael said.

I could tell from the stubborn look on his face that he wasn't going to take no for an answer.

Michael secured one end of a rope to a large rock, then tied the other end around Tyler, Becca, and himself. Slowly, my three friends started climbing down the steep wall while I watched, terrified.

Chapter 9

Fake pirates and real pirates

With Lilly's help, the Silver kids managed to reach the skull's eye. Now all we had to do was cross through the waterfall.

"Follow me!" Lilly said. She pulled me under the shower. We all came out on the other side coughing and spitting. Ptooey! Bats hate water!

Lilly pointed at a big hole in a rock. "There's a slide down there. All you have to do is to let go. Like this!" Without asking for my permission, she pushed me down, jumping in after me.

I could hear Lilly's laughter and Tyler's shouts as I plummeted into the unknown. Thankfully, we all landed safe and sound in a big puddle.

"First we walk through fountains," Tyler complained, his wet hair plastered over his eyes, "then the slide! What is this, some kind of amusement park? Well, I'm not amused at all!"

"Turn around, Tyler," Becca said. "There's another little surprise for you."

Tyler turned around and found himself standing before the *Ramshackle*. It wasn't tilted anymore, though. It was floating in the water.

"Is . . . is that Goldtooth's ship?" Tyler stuttered.

"Can we have a closer look?" Michael asked.

"As long as you're not too scared," Lilly said.

"Scared?" Tyler said. "Oh, no. I just love risking my life."

Ignoring their brother, Michael and Becca climbed aboard the ship. Tyler had no choice but to follow. The planks in the deck floor creaked ominously beneath our feet.

"That's far enough, Michael," Tyler said. "You saw the ship now. Can we go back? Michael! Michael where are you?"

A scream from behind our backs startled us.

"All men take their places! Raise the anchor!"

Shivering with fear, I turned around and breathed a sigh of relief. It was Michael, wearing a captain's uniform, holding the wheel and laughing. There was even a sword hanging from his belt.

"Where did you find those clothes?" Becca asked.

"There's a box full of them in the captain's

cabin," Michael said. "Come on, help yourselves!"

Michael talked us all into wearing pirate clothes. He even managed to make me wear a bandana.

Meanwhile, Lilly sat on the rail with a worried look on her face.

"What's wrong?" I asked.

"The sea level is rising," she said. "Maybe it's safer if we leave now."

Just then, Michael arrived back on the deck, holding a piece of yellowish paper. "Look what I found!" he said.

We could barely make out the words written on the half-torn piece of paper.

TAKE THE CROOK-POINTED
RAMSHACKLE
AND START LOOKING
LOOK DEEP, DEEP DOWN
AND YOU'LL FIND YOUR CROWN

"It looks like some sort of riddle," Becca said.

"You're right," Michael said. "But I don't understand what it's referring to."

"It's referring to my ship!" someone said from behind us.

We turned around slowly. The ghost of a real pirate was now holding the helm. A single golden tooth glimmered in his mouth. Around him stood the ghosts of more than a dozen buccaneers, all armed to the teeth and glaring at us.

No one dared to make a sound in front of Goldtooth and his crew of ghost pirates!

"That belongs to me, if you don't mind!" the pirate croaked, snatching the paper from Michael's hands.

"Look, Echo!" Lilly whispered. She pointed at the rising water that was quickly flooding the cave.

"Goodness me!" I said. "You mean . . ."

"This is the night of the ghost pirates!" Lilly said.

"To your stations, men!" Goldtooth bellowed. "Raise the anchor!"

Once again, the *Ramshackle* was ready to set sail for the open sea.

With us on board this time!

Chapter 10

Michael the diver

"Tie up these intruders!" the captain ordered. "I'll feed them to the fish when we're out at sea."

Lilly and I quickly flew to the top of the mast. My friends tried to scurry away as the ghostly pirates chased them. I'd never seen Tyler run so fast. Becca managed to throw a couple of kicks here and there.

"We have to do something!" Lilly said. "Otherwise your friends are done for!"

I looked down. Below, the captain was once again trying to make sense of the riddle.

I suddenly remembered what my Aunt Esmeralda always used to say. *"When a bat is full of fright, he'll fly faster than the light!"* Since my level of fear was off the scale, I was definitely going to be pretty fast. I zeroed in on the captain and snatched the piece of paper from his hands before he could even see me.

"Yippee! Go Echo!" Lilly cheered.

All the pirates raised their eyes and looked at me. "Catch that flying rat!" the captain ordered.

"How are we supposed to do that, boss?!" a short, bald pirate asked. "He can fly!"

Becca was the only one who understood what I was trying to do. "If you want your piece of paper back," she said to the captain, "you'll have to let us go!"

"Better yet," Michael added, "you'll have to take us with you!"

"What?" Tyler protested. "That's not better!"

"Why do you want to come?" Goldtooth asked. "Do you think it's a romantic boat trip?"

The pirates burst into thunderous laughter.

"We might be useful to you," Michael said.

"How exactly?" the captain asked. "Peeling potatoes?"

"We could recommend a very good dentist

for you," Tyler suggested, trying to be funny. Goldtooth glared at him.

"We could help find your treasure," Becca tried.

"We could even manage to solve the riddle written on that piece of paper!" Michael added. At that, all the pirates went silent.

"Hmm, maybe they want part of our treasure," the captain said. "But we've been searching for centuries, and every time we come back empty-handed. What harm could it do?"

Another pirate spoke up.

"I say we take them with us. They look like a bunch of clever kids!"

"Don't forget the bat!" another pirate said. "He showed a lot of guts snatching that paper."

Irritated, the captain interrupted them. "All right! They're coming with us!"

A triple hooray echoed in the cave.

"Echo!" Becca called me. "You can give the riddle back to the captain now."

I flew down to where the captain stood, but as I neared the deck, the unexpected happened. A gust of wind blew the piece of paper out of my hand and straight into the water!

Everyone rushed to the rail, but no one jumped.

"Come on, sailors!" Becca cried. "Someone has to get it before it sinks!"

Still nobody moved. Some looked at their feet, some whistled, and others cleaned their fingernails using a pocketknife.

"What's the matter with you?" Becca insisted. "Aren't you supposed to be seadogs?"

"Well, we are," the captain replied, keeping his eyes low. "But no pirate worth their name can swim. It's tradition."

"Well that tradition stinks!" Michael said. He suddenly jumped over the rail and dove into the water. He reached the piece of paper in a couple of strokes, and climbed back on board in a matter of seconds.

The captain started at him with his mouth wide open.

"Now we can raise the anchor!" Michael said.

Chapter 11

Red eyes and swollen noses

As the *Ramshackle* sailed through the waterfall and out of the cave, I saw the face of the island again. It really did look like a skull!

"Where are we heading, Captain?" the helmsman asked.

"We'll follow the ship's prow as usual," the captain replied.

"The ship's prow?" Tyler asked. "Why?"

"Because that's what the riddle says," the

captain replied. "'Take the crook-pointed ramshackle.' Now, my ship is called the *Ramshackle*. And look at her prow. Isn't it crooked enough for you? The riddle continues, 'And start looking, look deep, deep down, and you'll find your crown.' Now do you understand? We must go where the prow is pointing, and once we're there, we must start looking. That's simple, isn't it?"

"If it's so simple, why can't you find the treasure?" Becca asked.

"Bad luck!" the captain said. "It was all bad luck! Am I right, sailors?"

"You're right, Captain!" the pirates replied. "We've been very unlucky!"

"Do you remember that time when Ralph mended the sails, and they fell into pieces again?" the captain asked. "Bad luck!"

"I told you I couldn't sew!" one of the pirates said.

"And who remembers when we ate René's fish soup and everyone got sick?"

"Can you believe it? That fish was only a year old!" René the cook protested.

"What about the time we followed the prow all night long only to realize it was the stern? Bad luck!"

"I think someone turned the ship around that time!" the helmsman argued.

"We've had four hundred years of bad luck!" Goldtooth cried.

Michael walked up to Goldtooth, trying to reason with him. "Captain," he said, "is it possible that you misunderstood the riddle?"

"Misunderstood?" the captain asked. "What do you mean?"

"I mean that this might not be the full riddle," Michael said. "You see? The paper is torn along the edge."

"By the soul of a thousand pickled sardines!" Goldtooth exclaimed. "The boy is right! That means we're finished! Everything is lost!" The captain put his head on Michael's shoulder and burst into tears.

Seeing their captain cry, the other pirates followed suit. Even Tyler started sobbing hysterically.

We tried to make them feel better, but the pirates just kept sobbing and blowing their noses. There was no way to calm them down.

At the first light of dawn, the red-eyed captain ordered the ship's course be changed. The *Ramshackle* sailed silently back to the cave.

Once again, the treasure hunt had failed.

Chapter 12

The crooked truth

Not long after we arrived back at the cave, the
tide started to go down. The cave slowly dried up,
and the ship once again tilted on its side.

The captain lowered a gangplank for us, and
the whole crew crowded at the rail to say goodbye
for the last time.

"Dear friends," Goldtooth began, "we thank
you all for joining us and sharing in our hope and
disappointment on this unlucky night!"

Some of the pirates started crying again.

"In a few moments, we will go back to being only shadows," Goldtooth continued. "Another year will pass before we can try our luck once more. Farewell, my brave friends. Remember you, as we shall remember us! Or was it the other way around?"

Goodness me! One more word, and I would start weeping myself!

"Wait a minute!" Tyler interrupted. "Before we leave, I would like you to accept this small gift. It's just an old compass, but I think you might need it more than I do!"

The captain accepted the compass and wiped off a teardrop with his handkerchief. Then he looked more closely at it and turned up his nose. "But . . . by the stomach of Poseidon, its needle is crooked!"

Suddenly, Michael and I looked at each other. We had both thought the same thing!

"Its point is crooked," Michael muttered. "And it's also pretty ramshackle. Could it be . . ."

"The 'crook-pointed ramshackle.' Of course!" the captain exclaimed. "By all the top-gallant sails! Why didn't you tell me before, young man? Now it's too late!"

Growling with rage, Goldtooth flung the compass overboard.

"That's rude!" Becca scolded him. "Tyler was just trying to be nice."

She went to pick up the compass. As she got closer, she realized that a small turtle had appeared out of nowhere. It was shoving its little face into the open compass box.

"Twinkle!" Becca said, picking the turtle up.

In its mouth, the turtle held a folded piece of paper. "What do you have there?" Becca asked. "Let me see."

She unfolded the paper, and her face immediately brightened. "It's the other half of the riddle!" she exclaimed.

"Whaaat?" Captain Goldtooth yelped, immediately getting off the ship.

We put the two pieces of paper together. They matched perfectly! For the first time in four

TAKE THE CROOK-POINTED
RAMSHACKLE
AND START LOOKING
LOOK DEEP, DEEP DOWN
AND YOU'LL FIND YOUR CROWN

SEA COMPASS
DIG ALAS!
INTO THE CAVE
IF YOU ARE BRAVE.

centuries, the pirates were finally able to read the full riddle.

"What does it mean?" the captain asked.

"It means that the treasure is hidden in the cave!" Michael explained.

"And the point we have to follow is the compass's!" Tyler added, looking at the needle, which had finally started working.

"What is it pointing at? Where is it pointing?" the captain asked frantically.

"Down here!" Tyler answered. "Next to me!"

"Come on, men!" Goldtooth ordered. "Start digging! Maybe we can still make it before the sun comes up!"

Total chaos broke out. Some of the pirates were digging a hole, and others were filling it back up. Some were carrying sand away, and others were bringing it back!

"By Neptune's beard!" the captain bellowed. "You're a bunch of nitwits! Order! We need order!"

Even the Silver kids seemed helpless in the mayhem, and dawn was quickly closing in.

Just then, I remembered a lesson I'd learned from my cousin Limp Wing – the Rotating Flight! It's a special emergency maneuver used to take off from soft or swampy grounds. It works especially well when it's performed with a partner.

I turned to Lilly. "I have to ask you for a favour," I said.

Once I had told her my plan, she replied, "It will be just like dancing together again!"

We clasped hands, and on the count of three, started rotating at full speed.

By the time we were finished, the pirates were wiping dust from their eyes, but we had dug a deep hole in the sand. At the bottom, we could see the top of an old wooden chest.

Chapter 13

Angry and explosive

You won't believe what happened when we opened the chest.

The sun instantly flooded the cave, the water started rising, and the ship began to straighten.

The pirates hugged and cried at the same time. The curse that had confined them to that place was finally broken!

"Come on, sailors!" the captain ordered. "Get on board! We're leaving at last!"

They all stormed onto the ship. Once aboard, they started dancing and singing at the top of their lungs.

"Farewell, friends! Thanks for everything!" they called. "We'll never forget you!"

Goldtooth insisted on hugging us one by one. When he got to Lilly and me, he wouldn't stop kissing us! Finally, he told two of his men to carry the treasure on board.

Suddenly, we heard a loud bang. The walls of the cave shook, and big rocks started falling from above. A huge boulder fell right on top of the wooden chest!

"My treasure!" Goldtooth yelled.

More rocks kept falling. If the captain didn't get his ship out of there, he would be crushed just like the chest.

"Quick, you bunch of jellyfish!" he roared. "All men get to their oars! We have to get out of here!"

Lilly clutched my hand. "We have to go too!"

"But what about my friends? How are they going to get out?" I shouted.

At that exact moment, a huge piece of stone crumbled off the side of the cave, revealing the ocean outside.

Becca dashed towards the opening, holding Twinkle in one hand and dragging Tyler behind her with the other.

Only Michael was still inside the cave. I saw him reach down and pick up something from the floor of the cave. He stuck whatever it was in his pocket. Unfortunately, I was so busy watching Michael that I didn't see the rock falling from above. It smacked me right on the shoulder! Ouch!

It's a miracle I even managed to get out of there alive!

We reached the inlet where our boat was docked and quickly climbed aboard. Once we were a safe distance away, we turned to look back at the island. It was cloaked in mist and a column of white smoke.

"Hey! Look at that cloud over there!" Becca cried, pointing at the horizon. "It looks like a pirate ship!"

Sitting next to me, Lilly began to sob.

"What's wrong?" I asked.

"I haven't seen my family come out, Echo," she told me tearfully. "I have to go back and look for them."

Before I could stop her, she flew away, heading for the island.

I tried to go after her, but a jolt of pain in my shoulder stopped me.

* * *

Uncle Charlie was furious by the time we arrived back at the house. When he'd come home from his meeting and realized we were gone, he'd been worried out of his mind. He'd gone down to the dock and seen that the boat was missing as well. It hadn't taken him long to figure out that we'd taken it to go to the island.

He'd rushed to the harbour and tried to convince Cornelius to take him to the island. But once they heard the explosions coming from over there, neither Cornelius nor any other sailor had been willing to risk their lives and their boats.

"Were you trying to give me a heart attack?" Uncle Charlie screamed at us. "What were you doing over there all by yourselves?"

"We were looking for the treasure with the pirates, Uncle Charlie," Becca answered.

"Don't be a smart alec!" her uncle scolded her. "Tell me what happened over there! I want to know everything!"

Obviously, we didn't really include every detail.

Michael decided to skip the part about meeting Goldtooth and his crew of ghost pirates. And Becca didn't mention the treasure we had found and then lost again.

Tyler saved the biggest surprise for last. He opened his compass and pulled out two perfectly matched pieces of yellowed paper. It was the complete riddle, which he'd somehow taken from Captain Goldtooth!

"Where did you get that?" Becca asked.

"I found it in my Christmas stocking!" Tyler joked.

"It belongs to the captain!" Becca scolded him. "You should have left it to him."

"What captain?" Uncle Charlie asked.

"Oh, never mind, Uncle Charlie," Tyler said. "He's an old friend of mine." He handed the riddle to his uncle. "Could you give this to Cornelius? Tell him he was right about the compass. He'll understand."

Chapter 14

Ice Cream Island

The train for Fogville was scheduled to depart at 10 a.m. the next morning. I spent the whole night sitting on the window sill, waiting for Lilly to come back. By dawn, I was so exhausted that I drifted off to sleep. I had the strangest dream.

I dreamt it was my wedding day.

Lilly was wearing an amazing white dress, while I wore a midnight-blue suit and an elegant bow tie.

Uncle Procopius gave a very nice speech and finally turned to me, asking the big question.

"Echo, will you wake up? Wake up, Echo! We're going to miss the train!"

That wasn't Lilly speaking to me. It was Becca! The train was going to leave in twenty minutes, and I still hadn't heard from Lilly.

Surrounded by the familiar cloud of smoke, old Tripper left the house and headed for the station.

As soon as we could see the ocean, the four of us shouted in unison, "THE ISLAND!"

Uncle Charlie screeched to a halt and stared at the island in shock. The fog around Skull Island had disappeared, just like the legend said!

But it seemed the earthquake that had hit the island the night before had also changed its shape.

"It looks like an ice cream sundae!" Uncle
Charlie exclaimed.

"Maybe you could rename it that," Tyler said.
"Ice Cream Island! It would attract so many more
tourists!"

* * *

The train departed right on schedule.

"Farewell, sailors!" Uncle Charlie called, waving us off as the train started to pull out of the station. "Say hello to your mum and dad for me!"

While the others were waving goodbye to their uncle, I stared out of the window. I sighed sadly. Lilly was still nowhere to be seen.

"You know what my only regret is?" Tyler said. "The fact that we don't have anything to show for our adventure except for an old broken compass."

"And a turtle!" Becca said, letting Twinkle out of her bag.

"And a golden doubloon from the pirate's chest!" Michael added, showing us an old coin.

That must be what he picked up in the big cave, I realized.

I sighed again. I was the only one returning to Fogville empty-handed. And Lilly hadn't even dropped by to say goodbye.

I stared out of the window as the train chugged along. Just then, a little black bird shot past me.

I leaned out the window, trying to get a closer look, and the bird flew past me again. This time, it hit me square on the shoulder.

"Ouch! My shoulder!" I yelped. Suddenly, I realized it wasn't a black bird at all. It was a blue-eyed lady bat.

"Lilly!" I shouted in surprise. "Where on earth have you been?"

"You didn't think I could just let you leave without saying goodbye, did you?" she said.

"I was so worried about you!" I told her.

"I went back to the island to find my family, and, guess what, they're all okay!" Lilly said. "All thanks to you and your friends!" She reached out to hug me and kissed both of my cheeks.

I heard bells ringing in my head, and I felt like dancing!

"Uncle Procopius says hello," Lilly continued. "And he asked me to invite you to my next birthday party. Will you come?"

"Of course I will!" I replied.

"I'm counting on it!" She blushed and handed me a little piece of paper. "I can't wait to see you again."

"I can't wait to see you too!" I replied as she fluttered away.

I slumped back in my seat. Tyler started singing, "Echo has a girlfriend! Echo has a girlfriend!"

What was written on the note, you ask? Her address, of course!

What I didn't realize then was that writing a letter to Lilly would be harder than writing one of my scary adventure stories.

When we arrived back in Fogville, Mr and Mrs Silver met us at the train station. They were thrilled to have us back. The only thing Mr Silver wasn't so thrilled about was Twinkle. He kept complaining that every time we went somewhere, Becca came home with a new pet.

I couldn't agree more! If you ask me, one animal friend is plenty, especially if it's a bat!

Things are getting back to normal here in Fogville, as they do after all of our adventures. Becca spends hours talking to Twinkle. Personally, I don't understand what she finds so interesting about that turtle. At least when she talks to me, I talk back!

Michael is always busy polishing his golden doubloon. He spends practically all day staring at that thing!

And Tyler has set his mind to learning to cook fish, just like Uncle Charlie. He promised to make us "reef spaghetti" for dinner tonight. To tell you the truth, I'm not really looking forward to it.

In the meantime, I've been sitting in front of a piece of paper and looking for inspiration to write something to Lilly. You wouldn't think it would be so difficult for a writer! I started it in a poetic way:

My dearest Lilly,

The sky above is cold and dark, but in my heart, I feel a spark.

It burns brightly for you. I hope that you can feel it too!

Do you think she'll like it?

A "seafaring" goodbye from yours truly,

Echo

ABOUT THE AUTHOR

Roberto Pavanello is an accomplished children's author and teacher. He currently teaches Italian at school and is an expert in children's theatre. Pavanello has written many children's books, including *Dracula and the School of Vampires*, *Look I'm Calling the Shadow Man!*, and the Bat Pat series, which has been published in Spain, Belgium, Holland, Turkey, Brazil, Argentina, China, the United States, and now the United Kingdom as Echo and the Bat Pack. He is also the author of the Oscar & Co. series, as well as the Flambus Green books. Pavanello currently lives in Italy with his wife and three children.

GLOSSARY

antique very old object that is valuable because it is rare or beautiful

bearings sense of direction in relation to where things are

chaos total confusion

compass instrument for finding directions, with a magnetic needle that always points north

legend story handed down from earlier times. Legends are often based on fact, but they are not entirely true

ramshackle rickety or likely to fall apart

seafaring having to do with sailors or the sea

DISCUSSION QUESTIONS

1. Uncle Charlie only eats fish. Yuck! Personally, I prefer fruit flies. What's your favourite food? Talk about it.

2. After the earthquake, Skull Island completely changed shape. Now Tyler wants to rename it. Talk about some possible new names for the island.

3. This adventure started when the Silver kids and I went on a beach holiday. Talk about an interesting holiday you've taken. Where did you go? What did you see?

WRITING PROMPTS

1. Goldtooth and his crew spent years searching for their missing treasure. Write your own riddle to find the pirate's treasure. Make sure it's clear!

2. I'm a mystery writer. In fact, I wrote the story you just read! Now it's your turn to be a writer. Write a paragraph describing what adventure the Silver kids and I should go on next.

3. I could do with some help writing to Lilly. Imagine that Lilly is your penpal. Write a letter to keep in touch.

Check out more
Mysteries and
Adventures with
Echo and the Bat Pack